D1457025

WILLIAM JAMES

AMERICAN PHILOSOPHER, PSYCHOLOGIST, AND THEOLOGIAN

The Library of American Thinkers™

WILLIAM JAMES

AMERICAN PHILOSOPHER, PSYCHOLOGIST, AND THEOLOGIAN

Jennifer Viegas

rosen
central™

The Rosen Publishing Group, Inc., New York

To those readers who follow the example of William, Alice, and Henry James
by striving for purpose and integrity in their lives

Published in 2006 by The Rosen Publishing Group, Inc.
29 East 21st Street, New York, NY 10010

First Edition

Library of Congress Cataloging-in-Publication Data

Viegas, Jennifer, 1965–
William James: american philosopher, psychologist, and theologian/Jennifer Viegas.
    p. cm.–(The library of American thinkers)
Includes bibliographical references and index.
ISBN 1-4042-0505-5 (library bdg.)
1. James, William, 1842–1910. I. Title. II. Series.
B945.J24V54 2005
191–dc22

2005007723

36242060373418

Printed in China

On the cover: Background: A nineteenth-century lithograph of St. Paul's Chapel and the Broadway Stages in New York. Inset: William James in 1903.

CONTENTS

INTRODUCTION

"The greatest use of life is to spend it for something that will outlast it." –William James

M any scholars believe that William James was both America's greatest philosopher and the father of American psychology. These lofty titles might seem to hold little weight in today's world in which the name William James is often left out of lists that include familiar American historical figures. Nonetheless, James may very well have been the most influential American of the past few centuries. His extraordinary foresight and vision run like a current through virtually every aspect of American life today.

During James's time, there was a worldwide explosion of advances, particularly in the sciences. Two German

Born to a highly educated and successful family, William James would become one of America's most brilliant philosophers. James suffered from a number of health problems growing up. He would struggle with depression throughout his life, as did other members of his family. This struggle with depression may have contributed to his desire to learn about the human mind and behavior.

scientists, Matthias Schleiden and Theodor Schwann, theorized in the 1830s that individual cells make up all living things. Because the cells likely came from a single source way back in the history of the planet, the theory suggested that everything alive on Earth was linked together in a unified biological system. Just as a human is made of cells, so, too, is a plant or a dog. This notion was a radical departure from the view that humans dominated Earth and had no physical connection to nature.

Other scientists were finding out that certain mechanisms, or laws of nature, could explain how most occurrences in nature worked. For example, Russian chemist Dmitri Mendeleyev created the periodic table of the elements in 1869, which showed all of the known elements at the time. These elements could exist separately, like hydrogen gas. They could also combine to form other substances—for instance, a hydrogen atom can combine with two oxygen atoms to form water. In chemistry, Englishman John Dalton developed an idea that tiny particles, which later scientists identified as atoms, actually combined to form the elements. In physics, James P. Joule made important contributions to the laws of energy. Improved microscopes and study techniques led to discoveries in physiology and human behavior. By the mid-1800s, Austrian monk Gregor Mendel outlined the basic laws of genetics. Louis Pasteur of France made important advances in microbiology; he proved that microscopic germs cause disease.

One of the most influential discoveries emerged from the scientific expeditions of Charles Darwin. Darwin, a British naturalist, traversed the globe studying numerous plants and animals from many different countries. He concluded that all living things gradually change over time to adapt to their environments. Darwin called this process of change evolution, which he described in his groundbreaking book *On the Origin of Species*. At the heart of his theory was another process called natural selection. The reasoning behind natural selection is that the fittest organisms, or the ones that are best suited to their environments, will probably be the ones in any given population to survive and produce descendants.

Darwin's views were controversial in the nineteenth century, and are still a subject of debate today. The controversy emerged because some believed evolution and natural selection went against the creation account found in the Bible. Darwin's evidence, however, captivated many people. Darwinism intro-duced an entirely different way of thinking about life and about humans' place in the world. Even conservative religious leaders began to think and write about social and environ-mental issues related to the theory of evolution.

Advances in science and knowledge were being made at an incredible rate during William James's time. Suddenly people began to question the old teachings about science, humanity, religion, nature, and the meaning of life. It is nearly impossible

This humorous photograph shows the process of human evolution. When Charles Darwin first outlined the theory of natural selection in his groundbreaking work *On the Origin of Species*, published in 1859, it revolutionized the field of biology. Years before Darwin, a scientist named Jean-Baptiste Lamarck had also advanced theories about evolution, but they did not become popular. Still, Lamarck's work influenced Darwin.

to fathom how radical the changes were that occurred during this time in American history. A comparable period was several hundred years before, when people discovered that Earth was not the center of the universe.

For James, there was no barrier between religion and philosophy, music and psychology, or language and art. James thought that all of these subjects emerged from the overlap of nature, creation, and the human mind. Rather than focus on one particular subject, James took a multidisciplinary approach to his studies, producing work that would help to define American culture.

Consider what it means to be an American. At first, the answer might seem to be too varied and complex to even attempt a response. Americans may not see that their philosophical mind-set is often different from that of other cultures. In China, for example, fashion, theater, politics, architecture, music, and more of the people are all uniquely reflective of the Chinese system of values. The same holds true for Africa, the Middle East, Russia, and other parts of the world.

William James navigated the globe throughout his life. He rarely spent much time in any one place. Despite this, his background, traditions, and political views were rooted in American culture. William James was a quintessential American. He embodied the country's conservative past mixed with its quest for creating a new future.

While nearly 100 years have passed since James's death, the work that he began lives on. His writings and teachings permeate almost every facet of current American culture. Pop music, movies, novels, psychology, science, art, religion, and politics are just a few areas in which James's influence is still present. He did not invent a flashy machine or build a giant monument in his own image. His contributions were subtler, yet they continue to define and shape democracy, healthcare, popular culture, and what it means to be an American.

James was a creative visionary, but he also was very much a man of his time. His primary era was the nineteenth century, a time when America was still in its relative infancy. But, like an adolescent on the verge of becoming a teenager, the country was already becoming more independent.

William James was born during a hotbed of scientific advancement and philosophical and religious uncertainties. He absorbed the traditional and more modern scientific teachings of his time, which his remarkable and unique family introduced to him.

CHAPTER
1

THE JAMES FAMILY DYNASTY

William James came from a wealthy and influential family that included several famous individuals in addition to William. This great American dynasty actually began rather humbly in Ireland. William James's grandfather, William James Sr. (1771–1832), immigrated to the United States in 1789 to seek his fortune when he was only eighteen years old. His first main job was working as a clerk in a tobacco and cigar store. He became a partner in the business, which he expanded to include other products, such as hardware and groceries. William James Sr. used the

Completed in 1825, the Erie Canal connects the Great Lakes with the Atlantic Ocean. Although costly to build, the canal was a sound investment, helping New York's economy immensely. The canal was used less and less with the development of alternate shipping routes, but it is still open to recreational boats.

profits from his store to make a number of successful business and real estate deals. He was involved in the construction of a very profitable tobacco factory and operated a salt mining company out of New York.

Seemingly tireless and full of ambition, William James Sr. did not rest on his money and success as a businessman. He took an active role in his community and in American politics.

He served as vice president of the Albany Savings Bank in New York and as director of the New York State Bank of Albany. He then became a trustee of Union College and later was involved in negotiations to build the Erie Canal, a monumental waterway that stretches from Albany, New York, to Buffalo, New York.

In his personal life, William James Sr. held on to the conservative Catholic teachings of his family in Ireland, but he was also a very independent-minded individual. His work made him an extremely wealthy man. Some accounts say that he was the second-wealthiest person in all of New York. His wife and children, therefore, never wanted for material goods. Their household was full of nannies, important businessmen visiting the family, housekeepers, and more. Sometimes Henry James Sr. (1811–1882), William James Sr.'s son, felt lost amid the constant hustle and bustle.

HENRY JAMES SR.

Like his father, Henry James Sr. was a very religious man, but he also inherited his father's sense of independence and his tendency to question traditional views that stood in the way of his personal beliefs. He was a lively child who was active and curious. Early in his life, this adventurous spirit led to a horrific accident that would forever shape his future and that of his son William.

Henry James Sr. and his son Henry James Jr. pose in an 1854 daguerreotype. Like his father, Henry James Jr. was very studious. He would become one of America's greatest writers.

One day, while playing outside with his friends, Henry and his friends rolled up some balls of twine, soaked them in turpentine, and set them on fire. The game was to toss the fiery balls into the air and then to stomp them out with their feet. One of the balls fell into a stable full of hay, which then caught on fire. Young Henry tried to stomp it out, but the blaze overtook him. He was eventually rescued, but only after the fire had severely burned much of his body, including his right leg. His leg never did heal properly, so doctors had to amputate it. In the early 1800s, surgeons performed this procedure without any kind of anesthetic. Henry had the physical and mental strength to endure the pain, but the guilt surrounding his actions stayed with him for the rest of his life.

Henry James Sr.'s Religious Beliefs

In 1835, Henry James Sr. entered the prestigious Princeton Theological Seminary due to his interest in religion and to the fact that he hated the business world of his father. He also did not have the same ambitions and skills, perhaps because wealth did not hold the same incentive for Henry as it did for William Senior. Henry excelled in his studies at the seminary, but he did not agree with some of its conservative religious teachings. Instead, he looked to alternative views, of which there were many in the nineteenth century.

Henry first turned to Robert Sandeman. Sandeman's religious sect, Sandemanianism, arose out of one Protestant group. Sandeman opposed some of the old rituals and hierarchy associated with the Catholic Church. At this time, many masses were held in Latin, and families often sat in pews according to social rank. Sandeman did not emphasize a person's past or social status. Rather, he focused on what that individual believed. Therefore, according to Sandemanianism, a person who possessed true faith had an equal chance of being redeemed and receiving God's goodwill as someone who carefully followed every mandate of the Catholic Church. Since Henry had long been plagued by feelings of guilt over

Princeton Theological seminary was established in 1812 in Princeton, New Jersey. Henry James Sr. studied at the seminary in the 1830s, although he did not find the institution to be as radical as he would have liked. The building that housed the original seminary is now a student dormitory known as Alexander Hall.

his childhood accident, these views appealed to him and eased his mental anguish.

Swedenborgian Theology

Henry married and had five children. Like most wealthy families, they relied on hired help to care for the children and handle many of the household duties. Henry's wife, Mary, was a stable presence who kept a certain distance between herself and her children. Because of this, and because of women's lesser role in society during the 1800s, her children were primarily guided and influenced by Henry's views, which became more unorthodox as time went on.

Henry was captivated by the teachings of Emanuel Swedenborg (1688–1772). This Swedish mystic, scientist, and philosopher was raised by a theologian father who believed that personal feelings of love and having an individual sense of connection to God were more important than faith alone. Swedenborg respected his father's work, which influenced his own religious views and teachings.

Swedenborg began to develop his own views, however, through his interest in mysticism. Swedenborg believed that he could go into a trancelike state in which he could literally talk to biblical personages, such as Jesus and Moses, or angels and spirits. He felt that such encounters helped him to better understand scriptural teachings.

Henry found healing through Swedenborg. Swedenborg's followers advised Henry to think of his internal guilt and negative thoughts as little demons, entities that were not a part of Henry but instead somehow existed outside of him. Somehow Henry was then able to separate himself from his guilt. Although he suffered from panic attacks and depression throughout his life, he never lost faith in Emanuel Swedenborg, whom he lectured on and wrote about for many years.

Emanuel Swedenborg's father was a professor of theology at Sweden's Uppsala University and would later become a bishop. Emanuel Swedenborg was a brilliant scientist and inventor who began having religious visions later in his life. Turning his powerful mind toward theological matters, Swedenborg produced a number of books that would influence William James.

Swedenborg's influence on Henry was not limited to religious thought. The Swedish mystic was also a prominent scientist who made many discoveries in physics, geology, biology, chemistry, psychology, neuroscience, astronomy, and even in the study of dinosaurs. Henry aspired to learn about these fields as well, and he passed this interest on to his children.

Before the twentieth century, many scholars and wealthy individuals undertook such all-encompassing studies. Just as Renaissance men before them had an insatiable curiosity for literature, architecture, and the arts, many scholarly men of the eighteenth and nineteenth centuries dabbled in any number of different intellectual pursuits.

Henry James Jr.

Henry's namesake, Henry James Jr. (1843–1916), is perhaps the best-known member of the James family. He never married, devoting much of his life to writing and literature. Included among his published works are *The Wings of the Dove*, *The Turn of the Screw*, *The Ambassadors*, *The Golden Bowl*, *The Bostonians*, *The Europeans*, *Daisy Miller*, and *The Portrait of a Lady*. Many of these works have been adapted for modern movies and television programs. Henry Jr. also authored many other works, including essays, numerous pieces of literary criticism, and the prefaces to many well-known books. Henry James was one of America's greatest writers and most important literary theorists.

Henry Jr. remained close to his brother, William, throughout his life. As children, they developed a correspondence that lasted until their deaths. Although they were close, Henry and William had opposing views about life and literature. Many of Henry's books, such as *The Turn of the Screw*, are dark and psychologically complex. They certainly stood out among the popular romance novels of the day. In one letter to his brother dated October 22, 1905, William asked Henry to "write a new book, with no twilight or mustiness in the plot . . . no psychological commentaries, and absolute straightness in the style." Henry's response was that he would rather "descend to a dishonored grave."

OXFORD WORLD'S CLASSICS

HENRY JAMES
THE TURN OF THE SCREW
AND OTHER STORIES

Many of Henry James's novels have been made into films. Henry James's writing often dealt with psychological themes, and his work revolutionized American narrative fiction. Henry James was a prolific writer, and in addition to his fictional works he produced numerous pieces of literary criticism and essays. Although he wrote a number of plays, they were seldom performed.

ALICE JAMES

William's only sister, Alice James (1848–1892), did not enjoy the fame that her brothers achieved in their lifetimes. Her writings were discovered after her death and, in recent years, she has gained favor as an important feminist and journalist. Alice, like others in her family, suffered from serious anxiety, depression, and apparent mental illness. It is hard to say if these problems were brought on by genetics or the environment in which she was raised. Most historians think that the combination of her Victorian upbringing (women then were restricted to mundane roles) and some sort of biochemical imbalance was to blame for her suffering.

Alice was in and out of hospitals and treatment centers for much of her life. At times she contemplated suicide, and she was bedridden for long periods. Yet, no matter how much despair she felt, she always expressed her feelings beautifully in writing. According to *Genuine Reality* by Linda Simon, for example, she wrote that "I went down to the deep sea, its dark waters closed over me and I knew neither hope or peace."

A Family History of Mental Illness

Mental illness tormented Henry James Sr. and most, if not all, of his children. One of the earliest pieces of evidence of this, recounted in "Anxiety and Interpretation" by Tadd Ruetenik, comes from Henry Senior's own writings. In a document, he described what it felt like to experience a panic attack. In a letter he wrote,

> The thing had not lasted ten seconds before I felt myself a wreck; that is, reduced from a state of firm, vigorous, joyful manhood to one of almost helpless infancy. The only self-control I was capable of exerting was to keep my seat. I felt the greatest desire to run incontinently to the foot of the stairs and shout for help to my wife–to run to the roadside even, and appeal to the public to protect me.

Though mental illness is extremely difficult for anyone to bear, it was especially difficult to secure proper treatment for psychological disorders in the nineteenth century. Mentally ill people were often locked up in institutions and penitentiaries such as Blackwell's Island Lunatic Asylum in New York, shown here. This often made their conditions worse. Blackwell's Island was the predecessor of today's Riker's Island, one of the toughest prisons in the United States.

While doctors and psychologists still struggle to understand such bouts of panic, many studies suggest that these episodes are linked to chemical imbalances in the brain, heart problems, and hormones.

In the nineteenth century, mentally ill people were often locked up in institutions and considered social outcasts. Individuals who experienced even common mental health problems, such as depression, felt a sense of loneliness and self-hatred, as though they had committed a crime against themselves. Mental illness was often treated with strange procedures and medicines that could make a patient feel worse. Mind-altering drugs, many of which are now illegal, were often administered to patients. As a consequence, the condition often worsened or the patient became addicted to the medications.

GARTH AND ROBERTSON

Aside from Henry, William had two other brothers, Garth Wilkinson (1845–1883) and Robertson (1846–1910). Like others in their family, Garth and Robertson suffered from mental health problems. In an attempt to ease his feelings of depression, Robertson turned to alcohol. He struggled with his addiction for years after he fought in the Civil War. Both Garth and Robertson had tried to become successful cotton plantation farmers, but their crops failed. They were unable to achieve the business success of their grandfather and they did not seem to share the ambitious drive of their brother William.

WILLIAM

Born in 1842, William was the eldest of the James family children. Little record exists of William's boyhood, aside from some reminiscences authored by his brother Henry. In them,

Henry portrays a restless boy who desired attention and had a short temper, but who was talented and brilliant, even at a very young age. For example, the James children used to put on their own theatrical plays for themselves and their relatives. William often served as the lead director, writer, and star of these productions. Outside of such fun and games, Henry and his siblings looked to William for wisdom and guidance. William, at least in his own family, was a born leader. Considering that his family was one of the most prominent in New York, William's home life perhaps prepared him for his later associations with politicians, scientists, and scholars.

Chapter 2

Education and Influences

With their emotional upheavals, creativity, and thirst for knowledge, the members of the James family were products of the time in which they lived. Before the birth of William James and his siblings, America had engaged in the War of 1812 to protect the United States' shipping interests against interference from the United Kingdom. Most historians believe that neither side could claim a clear victory, but the war had a unifying effect on most of the United States, particularly in the north. It also led to a growing desire to break away from England, its mores, and its teachings.

BATTLE OF NEW ORLEANS
—AND DEATH OF MAJOR GENERAL PACKENHAM
On the 8th of January 1815.

The War of 1812 was a landmark in American history. The United States, a very young country at the time, defeated Great Britain, the world's preeminent military superpower. Although its defeat in the war didn't affect Great Britain very much, it was a very important victory for the United States. This painting shows the Battle of New Orleans, in which General Andrew Jackson defeated the British troops.

VICTORIANISM

A few decades after the War of 1812, Victoria (1819–1901) became queen of England. Queen Victoria ruled for sixty-three years, the longest reign in British history. During her reign, Britain's power grew due to the acquisition of numerous territories, including Egypt, Australia, Canada, and India. While America was in its cultural infancy and just beginning to define itself, Britain strengthened its worldwide position. In the past, cultural and political events in Britain and the rest of Europe influenced America.

On the face of it, the Victorian era was strong and stable. Read a book by Charles Dickens or Arthur Conan Doyle's Sherlock Holmes detective stories, however, and a darker side of Victorian England becomes evident. The rise of industry led to horrendous working conditions for middle- and lower-class individuals. Young children were often forced to work long hours at very low wages. Drug and alcohol abuse was rampant. Even the architecture and artwork of the time often combined sturdiness and stability with dark images of serpents and demons.

Henry James Sr. seemed to reflect the era's strength mixed with restlessness and doubt. His father disinherited him, but, upon William Sr.'s death, Henry sued and gained a sizable inheritance that made it possible for him to do pretty much what he pleased. In addition to his own religious and philosophical studies, he chose to focus on his family life. He wanted his children to be educated in the best possible manner. Intertwined

Working conditions were terrible in Victorian England. Work hours in factories were long, the factories themselves dangerous, and many of the laborers were young children. Although child labor is now illegal in England, it still persists in some areas of the globe.

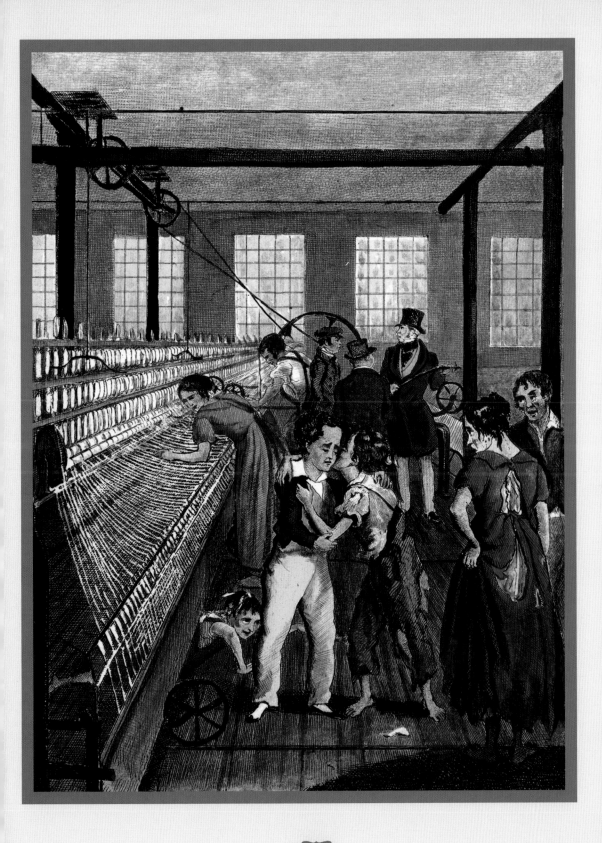

with this desire was the fact that whenever Henry Sr. felt restless or depressed, his reaction was to move to another state or even to another country. When he moved, the James family went with him.

AN INTERNATIONAL EDUCATION

In 1843, when William was just a year old, Henry Sr. moved his family to Europe. Desiring to learn the German language, Henry thought that he could master it more completely if he lived in Germany. After a short stay in Germany, Henry decided that the language barrier was preventing him from pursuing other intellectual pursuits, so he moved everyone to England.

By the late 1840s, Henry again grew restless. He moved back to the United States and settled in New York City. With five children, he now had a number of people who were under his financial and physical care. Some historians believe that he moved the family to New York in order to appease watchful relatives who wondered what the energetic Henry would be up to next.

From 1852 to 1855, William and his brothers were educated by a number of different tutors in many different schools. These schools were mostly small establishments that catered to wealthy families. One such school, Pulling Jenks, consisted of only a few rooms. There were only a few students for every teacher, however, so while William's social interactions with other children his age were limited, he received a lot of attention from his instructors. William showed an early interest in drawing and art, which he hoped to pursue as a career some day.

In the summer of 1855, Henry again decided to move, this time for the sake of his sons' educations. The family lived in homes in England and France. There, William again received private tutoring when he was not enrolled in small schools.

The size and quality of the schools meant that each student received a great deal of personalized guidance and mentoring. Students also did not have televisions, radios, and (in some cases) organized extracurricular sports to divert their attention both in and out of class. Education was integrated fully into the student's life, to the point where pupils and their families often had teachers over for dinner and enjoyed other social occasions together.

William particularly looked up to one teacher, identified in written accounts only by his last name. "Mr. Coe," as he was called, had an enormous head of thick, white hair and an imposing manner. As a teacher of art, he urged his students not to just read about it, but to draw all of the time, whether it be on small cards or large oil-painted panels. William, who already was interested in art, now devoted much of his free time to sketching and painting.

In 1858, when William was sixteen, his father announced that he planned to stay in London for a while before returning to New York. Letters to friends and relatives reveal that

Ralph Waldo Emerson, seen here in a photograph from 1875, was an American writer and philosopher and the guiding force behind the American transcendentalist movement. Emerson's 1836 essay *Nature* formed the foundation of transcendentalism, which opposed strict church laws. The transcendentalists promoted individualism and finding one's own relationship with God.

William felt most at home in New York. He found Paris to be cold and unwelcoming. London, with its frequent rainy days, also paled in comparison to the sunny days he had enjoyed when on vacation in the states along the Atlantic seaboard.

Henry Sr. changed his plans and left London early, which thrilled William. William's best friend at the time, John La Farge, returned from studying art in Paris and he, William, and the other James brothers enjoyed studying and catching up on the news in New York.

By 1859, William's father again wanted a change. He moved the family to Paris, then to Geneva, Switzerland, and later to Germany. Due to all of the international moves, William became fluent in five languages. He also learned how to mingle with the world's elite, and particularly with the prominent American writers and scholars who frequently socialized with his father. They too were well traveled and immersed in social circles around the globe. Such influential men included Ralph Waldo Emerson, Hermann Ludwig Ferdinand von Helmholtz, and Louis Agassiz.

RALPH WALDO EMERSON

Ralph Waldo Emerson (1803–1882) was a leading philosopher and author. As a friend of Henry James Sr.'s, William got to know Emerson as an individual and not just through his books, which include *Nature*, *Essays*, and *Spiritual Laws*. Emerson was originally a church pastor, but he quickly grew dissatisfied by the church's refusal to accept certain scientific findings and by what Emerson perceived was its disassociation with environmental processes.

When Emerson left his religious vocation, he helped create a new philosophical movement called transcendentalism. The transcendentalists believed that spirituality transcends, or triumphs over, the material world. Emerson believed that the ultimate fundamental reality, the truth that others found in the Bible, could never be fully known. Only through deep thought and calm meditation could a person find truth and his or her inner self. These ideas would later greatly influence the works of William James.

HERMANN VON HELMHOLTZ

The German physicist Hermann von Helmholtz (1821–1894) was another prominent figure in James's life. Today Helmholtz is most known for establishing the law of the conservation of energy. This law states that energy put into a system, such as gasoline into an engine, will not disappear—it simply turns into different forms of energy. In the example of an engine, some gas will help to run the engine while the rest will be converted to heat. William James studied physics and took an interest in Helmholtz's work. James was especially captivated by the German scientist's research on the nervous system.

Helmholtz was one of the first researchers to apply physiology to the nervous system through direct study. Through long hours of research and analysis, Helmholtz was able to measure the speed of nerve impulses. During his own career, William James continued to study the body and how it relates to the mind. Perhaps his interest came from his own frustration at not being able to cure, or even to understand,

William James attended Harvard University Medical School to study chemistry. Although he excelled in his studies, he had to take a lot of time off due to his frequent illnesses. James would eventually become a professor at Harvard. He spent a good portion of his life there, teaching a number of subjects.

the bouts of panic and depression he experienced, which were similar to those of his father's. Unlike Helmholtz, William disliked lab studies. He did some laboratory work over the course of his career, but usually he left the experimentation to other professors and students, preferring instead to teach and to write.

HARVARD UNIVERSITY

Despite his association with important scientists and philosophers, William still wanted to pursue a life as an artist and painter. This horrified his father, but William begged him to let him follow his dreams. From 1860 to 1861, William studied with the Newport, Rhode Island, painter William Morris Hunt. For reasons that remain unclear, these studies did not last for very long. After only about six months William decided that his future would be better if he studied at Harvard University. While it seems somewhat unusual today, William's father did not want his son to go. Stories about rowdy

At the time of the Civil War, one-third of the population of the American South were slaves. Slavery was an incredibly divisive issue in the United States; it nearly tore the country apart. Although many Northerners joined the Union Army to fight the South, James's health kept him from military service.

undergraduate partying and pranks had been in the papers. Yet again, William prevailed upon his father. Henry relented. In 1861, William entered the Lawrence Scientific School at Harvard to study chemistry.

CIVIL WAR

The same year that William entered Harvard, the Civil War broke out between America's Northern and Southern states. Suddenly the nationalism that had grown since the War of 1812 seemed like a distant memory. Divisive issues concerning slavery, cultural differences, religious beliefs, and economics threatened to dissolve the entire country. Many young men, including Garth and Robertson, enlisted to fight. William, however, suffered from a number of physical and mental health issues. He was, therefore, not as affected by the war as most men were and had the financial freedom to continue with his studies.

MEDICAL SCHOOL AND LOUIS AGASSIZ

At Harvard, chemistry did not hold William's interest. He decided to change his course of study. In 1864, he entered Harvard Medical School. While he certainly had the intellect to succeed in the school, William had inherited his father's restless nature. When an opportunity to join Louis Agassiz

Louis Agassiz was one of the first truly great American scientists. He studied zoology and geology, and he was the first person to theorize that the world had undergone an ice age. Agassiz would spend a good portion of his career studying glaciers. He was also notable for steadfastly refusing to believe in Darwin's theories of evolution.

(1807–1873) on an expedition to Brazil was offered, William jumped at the chance.

Agassiz was a Swiss naturalist who, like Darwin, studied various plants, animals, and fossils. Unlike Darwin, Agassiz did not believe in evolution. In fact, he was a staunch critic of Darwinism. Agassiz believed that species never changed over long periods.

William, however, did not seem too bothered by Agassiz's more conservative views. Instead, he relished the thought of traveling outside of Europe to see the Amazon. The trip unfortunately led to illness and another bout of severe depression for him. He resumed his studies at Harvard Medical School upon his return and received his medical degree in 1869. He was disenchanted with his future, however, which was possibly complicated by his lingering health problems. After three years of rest, William felt sufficiently recovered to begin work as an instructor in anatomy and physiology at Harvard.

A Popular Professor

By most accounts, William was beloved by his students. Like his writings, his class lectures at Harvard were energetic, heartfelt, humorous, and engaging, with many anecdotes thrown in from his extraordinary travels and personal life. In 1875, William began teaching psychology, which was then a fledgling field. That same year was a milestone for the young professor. William James became the first person to establish a laboratory devoted to experimental psychology. In fact, he was probably the first professor of psychology in the entire United States.

As if medicine and psychology were not enough, William became an instructor of anatomy and physiology at Harvard in 1873. In 1879, he began to teach philosophy, which led to yet another assistant professorship in that same subject a year later. During his years of teaching at Harvard, William lectured at other universities and at public gatherings.

While scientists such as Darwin could be booed off the stage due to their controversial views, William somehow captured the public sentiment of the time. He was neither a harsh conservative nor a fervent liberal. Like his father, he believed that religion and faith were important parts of life. His lectures often included stories about family pets and comical adventures. Although the public may not have been aware of it at the time, his work on psychology would permeate the American mind-set to such a strong degree that its influence is still felt today.

CHAPTER 3

THE PRINCIPLES OF PSYCHOLOGY

During William James's tenure at Harvard, he met and fell in love with a Boston schoolteacher and accomplished pianist named Alice Howe Gibbens (1849–1922). William, who was a lifelong proponent of personal choice and independence, nonetheless chose to marry someone whom his father felt was perfect for him. When William was thirty-four, his father attended a Radical Club meeting in Boston where he met Gibbens. Highly impressed by her, he returned home and told the family that he had just met William's future wife. It was lucky for William that he agreed with the choice.

Together William and Alice had five children and created a relatively happy home together. In Alice, James found someone in whom he could trust and confide. She was educated and intellectually curious, and they often spoke with each other about James's work and studies. Alice brought a sense of strength, calm, and stability to his life.

At the age of thirty-six, the same year that he married Alice, James began writing what was to become his greatest published work, *The Principles of Psychology*. His original plan was to teach and work on the book for a period of two years. That two years, however, wound up stretching to twelve. The work, published in 1890 and heralded as a "masterpiece" by Harvard University Press, was perhaps the first major American overview of psychology. While some of its contents now seem dated due to scientific advances that occurred long after James's death, a lot of the material remains fresh and relevant today.

A BRIEF HISTORY OF PSYCHOLOGY

The word "psychology" comes from the Greek words *psyche*, meaning "soul," and *logos*, meaning "word" or "knowledge." Modern psychology is the study of mind, behavior, and thought. Recent science has revealed that animals also possess unique patterns of thought, but such work was limited in James's day. He, therefore, largely focused on human behavior

Wilhelm Wundt is considered to be the father of experimental psychology, and his writings greatly influenced William James. Wundt took a very scientific approach to psychology, and many of his methods are still in use today. Along with William James, Wilhelm Wundt is considered to be one of the fathers of psychology.

and thought, although his work foreshadowed later findings about animal behavior.

As early as 1550 BC, a document called the Ebers papyrus contained a description of clinical depression. People in the sixteenth century were already becoming aware of mental health issues. However, superstition and traditional religious views of the time linked such mental health problems to invisible demons and ghouls.

From the sixteenth to the nineteenth centuries, academics believed that psychology was a field of study within philosophy. As a result, anything having to do with the mind and human behavior was rarely linked to the body and health issues.

Instead, human thought was viewed in an intangible, spiritual way. A breakthrough came in 1672 with the publication of a book called *Two Discourses on the Souls of Brutes*, which referenced psychology as a product of brain function, and not philosophy, magic, or religious miracle.

Many scientific advances came to light in the 1800s. During the midst of this new scientific revolution, German scientist Wilhelm Wundt (1832–1920) founded a laboratory devoted to psychology. James, who was fluent in German, read all of Wundt's works and was greatly influenced by them. Both men studied religion and metaphysics, but they had concluded that psychology should exist on its own as a separate field of study. This separation was earth-shattering for the time, comparable to Darwin's revolutionary discoveries. Although parallels exist between Wundt's teachings and those of James's, James formulated his own ideas based on his beliefs and American values.

Stream of Consciousness

The phrase "stream of consciousness" is common today. It is used to describe a literary technique as well as the way in which people think. James's work on stream of consciousness changed the way we view ourselves.

Before *The Principles of Psychology* was published, scientists and philosophers offered all sorts of explanations for how humans think. One theory said that thoughts existed in neither time

Jack Kerouac, seen here in a 1957 photograph, was one of America's most revolutionary writers. Kerouac was a member of the beat generation, a group of young bohemian writers and artists who were active from the late 1940s to the early 1960s. In 1957, Kerouac published his stream-of-consciousness novel *On the Road*, which he wrote nonstop over a three-week period.

nor place. Yet another said that thoughts stopped and started, as though an awake person could shut them off and then turn them on. James disagreed with these theories and instead likened consciousness to a stream that was always flowing and changing. A person may think about the same thing repeatedly, but the thoughts are slightly different each time, probably due to changes in experience and that individual's environment.

A fictional example of a stream of consciousness is, "I have to hurry to catch the bus to school today. Oh, there's my lunch. Ow, my leg hurts from when the soccer ball hit me yesterday. Now where is my book bag?" This rather basic example illustrates how our thoughts do not always focus on the same thing, but that they join in a flow over any given period.

The concept of stream of consciousness especially appealed to many writers who were trying to capture reality in their books. Edgar Allan Poe, for example, chronicled the disjointed stream of thoughts of one of his characters in his novel *The Narrative of Arthur Gordon Pym of Nantucket*. Virginia Woolf (1882–1941) also utilized stream of consciousness in her novel *Mrs. Dalloway*. In more recent times, Jack Kerouac (1922–1969) used the technique in his popular travel narrative *On the Road*.

AMERICAN INDIVIDUALISM

William James believed that human thought is personal. What one person thinks is unique to that human, based on whatever experiences and situations that individual has had throughout his or her life. James also believed that a person owns experiences, meaning that the memory of certain events and feelings again is unique to every individual. For example, a teacher could ask a roomful of students to imagine themselves relaxing on a sunny beach. While each person would likely visualize similar things, such as sand, sun, and water, other aspects would vary based on whatever prior experiences the individual had enjoyed at a beach.

The idea that thought is personal seems so commonplace today that we take it for granted. However, William James was one of the first people to formulate this notion. This is a very American notion. In some countries, people view themselves as part of a collective whole, in which the individual pales in comparison to the needs of a larger group. In America, acknowledgement of the individual is key to fundamental rights, such as freedom and the ability to pursue happiness. What William James proposed was fully compatible with ideals expressed in great American documents such as the Declaration of Independence. It is no wonder that James's book was so popular in America during his lifetime and still affects us today.

SELECTIVE CONSCIOUSNESS

Another important theory in *The Principles of Psychology* concerns human consciousness. According to James, human consciousness

William James's revolutionary approach to thinking about the human mind combined psychology and physiology. His studies led him to believe that human beings often operate instinctually, much in the same way that animals do. At the same time, he also believed that human beings possess free will.

is a force that continuously organizes and controls what it perceives. Each person controls these thoughts based on instinct and choices founded on personal interests and experiences. Like Darwin, James saw the connection between humans and other animals. People, like animals, sometimes act on instinct. If a person waves a hand near a dog's eyes, for example, the dog will likely blink or flinch in an instinctual move to ward off a perceived danger. Humans will do the same thing. James wrote in *The Principles of Psychology* that "instincts of animals are ransacked to throw light on our own," and he dismissed the idea that "man differs from lower creatures by the almost total absence of instincts."

James went on to say that humans are not entirely governed by instinct. Over time, instincts mix with experiences and memories that wind up changing how a person reacts. These experiences can lead to changed expectations, which can alter the original instinctual response. For example, a child could be afraid of dogs due to a bad experience when one bit him. Whenever he now sees a dog, he is fearful. Over time, he is gradually introduced to friendlier dogs. He does not forget the bad experience, but his instinct to be afraid of all dogs changes somewhat.

THE COGNITIVE NATURE OF THOUGHT

James outlined the idea that thought is cognitive, meaning that it concerns something other than itself. In other words, while we have some control, whether instinctual or selective, over our perceptions, the outside world is what mostly governs our thoughts. Even if a person thinks about thinking, he or she has to do so in reference to some kind of experience or material object found in the outside world. Our thoughts, therefore, are largely shaped by the world in which we live.

By acknowledging that humans do not have full control over the subject matter of their thoughts, James asserted that all creation exists in a world that is not entirely of human or animal making. Some other force must be at work. He did not rule out certain religious teachings, but he did believe that a person's words and actions could, to some extent, change what goes on in the rest of the world. In a way, James was reflecting the conflict between his grandfather's remarkable independence and power, and his own father's feelings of helplessness in light of his childhood accident. James knew that although his predisposition to depression was somewhat out of his control, he could succeed in making an effort to change his way of thinking for the better. Today, scientists realize that depression can result from biochemical imbalances in the brain, which James likely inherited from his father's side of the family.

INTROSPECTION

James believed in the validity of introspection. When a person becomes introspective, he or she dwells upon personal thoughts and feelings. Introspection is a form of self-analysis. For example, a student may say something hurtful to a friend and then regret it. While the student may be too embarrassed to admit the mistake, he or she might later think about why the insult was said, and what prompted such negative behavior.

James admitted in *The Principles of Psychology* that intro-spection is "difficult and fallible," but he still believed that it could be a valuable tool for mental health practitioners, who were rare in the nineteenth century. Introspection allows a person to think back on thoughts and behavior with new

information and experiences. Going back to the example of the student, that person learned the hard way that an insult can hurt another. This, in turn, could lead to problems for the person who made the negative comment. Through introspection, the student could then figure out what mistakes might have been made and then apply these lessons to future behavior.

PSYCHOANALYSIS

William James did not invent psychoanalysis. The invention of this psychological treatment, which is still popular today, is attributed to the Viennese doctor Sigmund Freud (1856–1939). Freud developed his theories in the 1890s, after James's book on psychology had been published. Freud certainly would have been familiar with James and his work, which may have inspired the development of psychoanalysis.

Psychoanalysis combines introspection with the presence of an educated listener. A person undergoing psychoanalysis

Sigmund Freud, seen here with his wife, Martha, was the father of modern psychoanalysis. He began his career focusing on neurology, but soon became involved in the field of psychology. At the start of Freud's career, most people thought that human beings had control over their thoughts and actions. Freud did not think this was the case. He believed that the unconscious mind, or subconscious, was responsible for much of human thinking and action.

talks to an analyst, who listens and only interrupts to ask certain pointed questions. The goal of the analyst is to detect patterns of thoughts within the individual's stream of consciousness. These thought patterns may lead to negative behavior. In addition, many analysts believe that when a person becomes introspective aloud, unconscious thoughts can sometimes come to the surface. A student, for example, may have trouble getting along with a certain classmate, but she is not sure why. Psychoanalysis could reveal that the classmate reminds her of someone hurtful from her past, someone whom she had long since seemingly forgotten.

AMERICAN FREEDOM

Overall, *The Principles of Psychology* suggests that people inhabit a free world in which, despite many limitations, individuals can exert some control over their own thoughts. These thoughts, in turn, can lead to actions that can change the lives of others, and the world around them. James rejected prior theories on destiny and determinism, which suggested that humanity is not free, but is instead completely ruled by outside forces. James's belief in freedom was consistent with American democracy. An ideal form of democracy supports individualism. It upholds the individual's right to be different. Most important, it celebrates freedom. Although perhaps unintentional, James's masterwork on psychology is, like the author himself, quintessentially American. His views continue to influence and to define American politics and culture, and it would be nearly impossible to measure James's lasting impact on modern psychology and mental health care without them.

CHAPTER 4

SCHOOLS OF THOUGHT

History books cover William James for his contribution to psychology alone, but there was another, equally important side to his work—philosophy. Today many scholars regard William James as being one of America's foremost philosophers. He was one of the founders of what could be America's only primary school of philosophy.

Philosophy, science, and psychology are different disciplines that require very different approaches. James took an equal interest in all three. His knowledge of these subjects is reflected in all of his works and it helped to shape his theories and findings.

PHILOSOPHY

The word "philosophy" comes from Greek, meaning "love of reason." Since the beginning of human civilization, people have been trying to understand the meaning of reality, knowledge, life, beauty, morality, and truth. Philosophers do not always rely upon scientific or religious beliefs and teachings to formulate their ideas. Philosophy has its own unique methods of inquiry, relying on human discourse, questions, debates, and logic.

Philosophy has flourished for thousands of years, but there was a strong revival of interest in it during the 1800s, perhaps because of all the new scientific discoveries taking place. While philosophers did not test their theories with scientific methods, discoveries about scientific matters such as cells, evolution, and genetics led to a lot of philosophical questioning in the nineteenth century. Since physical evidence did not always seem to support religious teachings, philosophers struggled with issues that were previously thought to have been settled, such as existence, values, humanity, and nature.

PRAGMATISM

Pragmatism refers to a school of philosophy that began in the United States toward the end of the nineteenth century. William James was one of its founders. Many experts now believe that pragmatism is the only uniquely American school of philosophy.

The school largely evolved out of the Metaphysical Club, which was a club in Massachusetts during the 1800s, whose members mostly consisted of Harvard professors and famous academics. After teaching his classes at Harvard, James would often join his friends and colleagues at the club to discuss philosophy and the pressing issues of the day. Darwinism was a driving force behind discussions at the Metaphysical Club. It became popular with James and his colleagues because it held that life could be an ongoing process that may not always be explained by theological views of history.

While there are different types of pragmatists, most believe that truth, or the property of being in accord with fact or reality, comes from consequence, practicality, and usefulness. This was a very American concept. In Britain, for example, history and tradition played a more important role in defining political decisions and social mores. If a person was born into royalty, he or she was assumed to be the best suited for leadership. A pragmatist might argue that such a system is not practical unless the majority believes in it.

Pragmatists often believe that, after all possible effort has been made to gather information on an issue, it is better for a person to make a clear-cut decision as opposed to leaving the matter open-ended. William James, for example, stated

The founder of pragmatism, Charles Peirce, published two books during his lifetime, as well as a number of papers in academic journals. Like many American philosophers, Peirce was born in New England and studied at Harvard, where his father was a professor. Pragmatism would become one of the most significant American schools of philosophy.

that even when individuals said they could not make up their minds, that in itself constituted a decision—a decision not to decide.

Having a will to believe in something or someone was critical to pragmatists. Indecisiveness was viewed as laziness or simply not caring, because life is full of choices and different possible paths. Perhaps this notion was especially relevant to William because, due to his privilege, ability to travel, and exposure to so many important people during his lifetime, he found himself with countless possible choices and directions that he could have taken. It is no wonder that he somewhat went against tradition by practicing what he preached. He wound up striving for excellence in so many different fields of study.

Aside from possible opposition to traditional views, pragmatism also evolved to counter the rationalist movement, which was popular in the nineteenth century. Rationalism is a philosophy that believes that truth comes from reason and factual analysis. Pragmatists argue that even the notion of "fact" can be debated. They believe that humans create their own collective reality, based on thought, intellect, and experience.

Charles Peirce

William James credited Charles Peirce (1839–1914) as being the founder of pragmatism. Peirce (pronounced "purse"), like

James, was born into a family of intellectuals. His father was a professor of astronomy and mathematics at Harvard. Peirce began his career as a scientist but became more interested in philosophy over time. Peirce also suffered from mental health problems, including depression.

Peirce was a friend and a mentor to James, who greatly admired his work. Both men were interested in science as well as philosophy, and they tried to apply their knowledge of each field to the other. In addition to his written works on pragmatism, Peirce is best known today for developing systems of modern logic. These systems were applied to early computer program development, so there is a surprising link between Peirce's nineteenth-century theories and today's modern technologies. He even described the "on-and-off" properties of switches in terms of logic. Electrical switches can be analyzed in writing through logic problems. This is called a logic gate, a concept that Peirce helped to create. To formulate such an analysis, each circuit can be thought of as either "on" or "off." In some situations, both circuits have to be on for there to be any output of electricity. In other situations, only one switch has to be on. Such logic gates allow for many different options with only two states, "on" and "off." That idea later was applied to electricity in the development of computer chips. Peirce also developed graphs that are still used today in calculus.

Pragmatism and radical empiricism are uniquely American schools of thought. There was a great sense of nationalism in America during the mid-1800s, a period of time sometimes referred to as the American Renaissance. The ideas put forth by the Founding Fathers in the Declaration of Independence had created a democratic country, and the writings of American thinkers such as William James helped form the philosophy of the young nation.

Radical Empiricism

Peirce may get most of the credit for pragmatism, but James created his own unique school of philosophy called radical empiricism. Radical empiricism is a philosophical school within pragmatism. The word "empiricism" refers to the practice of relying upon observation and experience. Empiricism itself was a movement that existed before James came on the scene. Empiricists believed that experience was a product of reality. Following a more pragmatic approach, James believed that experience did not have to be linked to reality because experiences themselves formed reality. He said that experiences contain knowledge and that this knowledge is associated with memory. For example, a student picks up a paper cup containing boiling water and burns his hand. The next time he picks up a cup of boiling water, he knows to place a holder or a napkin around it. Memory of the past experience created the reality in his mind that the liquid was hot. James's empiricism was "radical" because it emphasized experience as opposed to more scientific or rational explanations.

This theory somewhat paralleled his concept of stream of consciousness. Like thoughts in a stream of consciousness, James believed that even disjointed experiences were ultimately connected, and that a past experience could affect a future one.

EPISTEMOLOGY

Epistemology is another branch of philosophy. The term derives from a combination of Greek words. *Episteme* is Greek for "science," and *logos* means "word" or "explanation." Epistemology refers to the study of nature, origin, and scope of knowledge. Knowledge is not always linked to truth, so epistemology calls into question virtually every field of study. For example, for years people believed that all planets revolved around Earth. When that was scientifically disproved, the former knowledge about planetary movements was said to have been incorrect.

William James wrote and lectured about his own views concerning epistemology. James put a lot of emphasis on the meaning of truth. He said in his lecture "Pragmatism's Conception of Truth" that "true ideas lead us into useful verbal and conceptual quarters as well as directly up to useful sensible termini. They lead to consistency, stability, flowing human intercourse . . . [but] all true processes must lead to the face of directly verifying sensible experiences somewhere." In other words, James could not believe something to be true simply because it was supported by preconceived notions rooted in tradition, religion, or even science. The truth must have a practical, pragmatic element in order for it to be justified. It must somehow serve the needs of the individual and society.

Again, this was a very American viewpoint. It was in keeping with the Declaration of Independence, which includes the phrase, "We hold these truths to be self-evident," regarding those stated in the document. In that case, truth was determined based on value and experience, not on the commands issued by the British government.

During the 1800s, America was still in its infancy as a country, so James's beliefs helped to distinguish the nation from its former motherland, England. Truth was to come not from tradition, as it had in many parts of Europe, nor was it always to arise from religion. The truth, according to James, must instead come from the people and their own beliefs and experiences. Like experiences and stream of consciousness, truth was a phenomenon that was subject to change. James believed it was not absolute and eternal, as many theologians and philosophers had previously stated.

THE THEORY OF EMOTION

In addition to truth, James helped to create a theory of emotion. He concluded that emotion is how the mind perceives something that affects the body and senses. He would often cite an example involving a bear. If a person sees a bear, he does not fear it and then run, according to James. Instead, James believed that the person sees the bear and runs, so consequently the person fears the bear. The subtle difference is that fear is a

Starry Night, by the Dutch painter Vincent van Gogh, is an example of a work of art that forsakes realism in order to directly express emotion. Van Gogh's unconventional style did not win him many admirers during his lifetime, although he is now considered to be one of the greatest European painters. *Starry Night* shows the view van Gogh had out of the window of his room in the psychiatric center at Monastery Saint-Paul de Mausole in France.

product of the mind's perception. Fear is the emotion James mentioned in this example, but he believed the theory could hold true for all emotions.

AESTHETICS

James's theories resulted in later developments in aesthetics, which is a branch of philosophy that concerns the nature of beauty, art, and how people judge and value objects. He thought that enjoyment of anything, such as a painting, music, dance, or even the physical appearance of another person, could lead to both primal and secondary pleasures. These secondary pleasures were determined by the person's prior experiences.

During the nineteenth century, people debated the merits of classic art versus the new "romantic" art that put more emphasis on the direct expression of emotions. James put his theory of emotion to practice when he considered the different ways that individuals can view art. He wrote in *The Principles of Psychology*,

> Complex suggestiveness, the awakening of vistas of memory and association, and the stirring of our flesh with picturesque mystery and gloom, make a work of art romantic. The classic taste brands these effects as coarse and tawdry, and prefers the naked beauty of the optical and auditory sensations, unadorned with frippery or foliage. To the romantic mind, on the contrary, the immediate beauty of these sensations seems dry and thin. I am of course not discussing which view is right, but only showing that the discrimination between the primary feeling of beauty, as a pure incoming sensible quality, and the secondary emotions which are grafted thereupon, is one that must be made.

"GREAT MEN, GREAT THOUGHTS AND THE ENVIRONMENT"

In 1880, James gave a famous lecture for the Harvard Natural History Society. He later published the lecture in that year's October issue of the *Atlantic Monthly*. The paper was entitled "Great Men, Great Thoughts and the Environment," and it was written in a manner that would appeal to a broad audience. Although written with James's usual light humorous touch and deft intellect, the paper addresses some large questions, such as what can explain cause and effect, why anything happens in this world, and why people and countries are so different from each other.

In the paper, James presents an example where a friend of his family's happily dined with him at a large gathering. Some months later, this same man slipped and fell on some ice and died. James somewhat humorously suggested that the two events were linked, but then concluded that the man's life before the slip and the slip itself were not the real causes of his death. Instead the blame could be attributed to "the conditions which engendered the slip," one of which just happened to be the poor man's dinner with James several months beforehand.

James further explained in "Great Men, Great Thoughts and the Environment" that happenings, such as the man's slip, and differences, such as changes at Harvard over thirty

The *Atlantic Monthly* was founded by a group of American writers, including Ralph Waldo Emerson, in 1857. The first issue of the magazine came out in the November of that year and was greatly successful. Over the years, James's work was published in a number of issues of the *Atlantic Monthly*.

years, are "due to accumulated influences of individuals, of their examples, their initiatives, and their decisions." People, therefore, have enormous control over their own lives and the lives of those around them. Again, this was a very American approach to philosophy, as many Americans value the idea that people are free and have the ability to improve the quality of their lives based on initiative and hard work.

"Great Men, Great Thoughts and the Environment" was James's philosophical counterpart to Charles Darwin's work on evolution. James himself, in fact, states in the paper that such a connection exists between his theories and those of Darwin. In the paper he wrote, "A remarkable parallel, which

I think has never been noticed, obtains between the facts of social evolution on the one hand, and of zoological evolution as expounded by Mr. Darwin on the other." James believed that societies, and even countries like America, evolved over time, just as Darwin said plants and animals did. As a result, anyone who was alive in James's day had just as much power to change the system as those who were alive when the country was founded.

James's Theories Applied

The views that James expressed about knowledge, empiricism, pragmatism, truth, and more do not exist only on paper or as the stuff of philosophical musings. James believed that ideas, especially pragmatism, could be used to resolve disputes between groups or individuals. For example, one politician believes that his country should go to war, while another disagrees. According to James, these individuals should first determine if there are any practical differences between their beliefs. In this example, the differences would be profound, as going to war, or not, would have dramatically different consequences.

The pragmatic approach would next have the men examine the consequences of each of their proposed decisions. These consequences would have to be applied to imagined future experience, such as, "If we go to war, then _____ will happen."

Analysis of both lists of possible consequences could then lead to the most practical, or pragmatic, approach that either side should take. James's approach runs counter to decisions based on existing theological truths, such as going to war for the sake of religious beliefs. It also opposes decisions based on personal emotions, such as hatred or favoritism. In theory, pragmatism offers a fair and unbiased way to resolve disputes, particularly between individuals or groups. The idea particularly gained favor in America, where people represent various religious, ethnic, and economic backgrounds. With a pragmatic approach, everyone's ideas should have an equivalent chance of acceptance.

Is pragmatism, as the name suggests, practical? Many adherents today would say yes. However, in William James's day, most of the people within his social circles, even on an international scale, came from similar backgrounds, with educations rooted in comparable teachings and shared values. When he debated issues with them, the pragmatic approach often worked. Pragmatism remains an ever possible, yet elusive, goal in America, which has been challenged by divisiveness on many political and ethical matters.

CHAPTER 5

JAMES BRIDGES THE RELIGION-SCIENCE GAP

William James inherited a passionate interest in religion from his father and grandfather. Both men spent a great deal of time studying world religions, lecturing about religion, authoring newspaper and journal articles on the subject, and writing related books. William James's greatest work about religion was a book titled *The Varieties of Religious Experience*. It is astonishing to think that such a work could come from the same mind that just twelve years earlier produced the then-definitive text on psychology. There was seemingly no limit to James's intellectual curiosities and abilities.

James was a very religious man, and he wrote frequently on the philosophy of religion. He believed in mystical experiences and sought to have them himself. In pursuing a true mystical experience, he came to believe that there are many different forms of human consciousness. This circa 1860 photograph shows the Old Christ Church in Alexandria, Virginia.

Because James had such a worldly education involving numerous languages, disciplines, and viewpoints, he did not see barriers between subjects, as many people do today. In his opinion, religion was just as important as any science, if not more so, and it could be applied to science and medicine without compromising his other beliefs on individual truths and freedoms.

James believed that religious experiences represented an enhanced, revealing view of a person's true values and desires. Somewhat like a dream state, these experiences could cut through the everyday chitchat within a person's consciousness to determine core values. James felt that psychologists should pay special attention to an individual's accounts of his or her own religious experiences in order to better understand that person.

NINETEENTH-CENTURY MYSTICISM

When reading James's accounts of religious experience, it is important to remember that mysticism, in addition to traditional religious views, was popular and accepted, particularly among the American and European elite. Mysticism refers to a belief that, through intuition or even direct communication with spirits or otherworldly phenomena, a person can become closer to God or to gaining some sense of spiritual fulfillment. Mysticism still exists today, but not to the extent that it did in the 1800s.

During the nineteenth century, people did not have televisions or radios to occupy their time in the evenings. It was common for families, particularly among the wealthy, to entertain in the evenings with dinner parties and other social gatherings. Séances, in which people would gather in hopes of communicating with the deceased, grew in popularity. A number of people claimed to be psychic mediums who

Catholic churchgoers attend Mass in New York City's Church of Our Lady of the Rosary. During James's time, Catholic Mass was very traditional. The priest delivered the service in Latin, the priest did not face the congregation, and the congregation did not join in many of the church prayers. Although he was interested in many different religions, James thought that most religions placed too much emphasis on tradition.

could go into trances and communicate with the dead. Henry James Sr. believed in such powers, as he was a staunch follower of Emanuel Swedenborg and his mystic practices. William James was not a Swedenborgian, but he did often visit psychic mediums, many of whom were later proven to be fakes who were just taking advantage of their wealthy patrons. Regardless, William used mystics in an attempt to gain religious enlightenment.

SCIENCE AND RELIGION

James, like many of his contemporaries, was curious about different religions and practices, but his core beliefs were rooted in Christian teachings. Both Catholic and Protestant churches at the time were much more traditional than they are now, in terms of the length of mass times, the language used (usually Latin in Catholic churches), adherence to the sacraments, and in other ways. James thought that too much emphasis was placed on the institutions and not the religious issues themselves. Through his work in philosophy and religion, he hoped to lessen the focus on church structure and tradition by reminding people of the big issues that religions addressed.

James was clearly interested in science and the many discoveries of his time, which he spent many years studying and,

Muslims pray facing Mecca at the Islamic Cultural Center of New York in New York City on the first day of the holy month of Ramadan. Islam is the fastest-growing religion in the world, and the second-largest, behind Christianity. James himself was a Christian who thought that people benefited from the practice of any religion.

later, teaching. Many scientists moved away from religion as a means of explaining the world, its origins, and existence itself. James, however, maintained that religion was not obsolete. He said that the value of religion came down to a purely individualized point of view. Religion, he said, was "an essential organ of our life, performing a function which no other portion of our nature can so successfully fulfill."

FAITH

The prevailing point of *The Varieties of Religious Experience* concerns faith. James felt that faith was a necessary part of life. It fit into his views on consciousness and experience because he claimed that faith, which he also termed "over-beliefs," could help to interpret the shared experience and history of any given two individuals or groups. This faith, or over-belief, is something that cannot be proved by scientific or rational means.

James's views on hope were consistent with his belief that humans exert control over their own thoughts. James extensively studied religious texts from all over the world and determined that hope was one of the key expressions of virtually all religious faiths. Most religions offer believers the encouragement that life has meaning and purpose. They also often encourage followers to believe that the future can be better than the past, particularly if the individual takes steps in the right direction to achieve desired goals.

James referred to something he called "the strenuous mood," which he felt within himself. This mood was an impulse to find passion and meaning in life. It was also a desire to end personal suffering, as well as to ease the suffering of others. It created a drive in him to pursue his talents to their fullest. This "strenuous mood" also emboldened him to humanize existence, meaning that he desired to interpret experience and his environment in human terms that valued diversity and difference.

Some of James's most important work bridged the gap between science and religion. The fact that he was a scientist did not keep him from believing in things that could not be scientifically proven. His view of religion was an optimistic one, and he thought that belief was an important factor in a person's happiness.

James believed that all religions should be respected and taken seriously. James was careful not to mention specific names of religions, but instead used generic terms that could apply to any belief system worldwide. Likely, this was because he had friendships and business associations with people from all over the globe. James wrote in *The Varieties of Religious Experience* that

There must be something solemn, serious, and tender about any attitude which we denominate religious. If glad, it must not grin or snicker, if sad, it must not scream or curse. It is precisely as being solemn experiences that I wish to interest you in religious experiences . . .

The divine shall mean for us only such a primal reality as the individual feels impelled to respond to solemnly and gravely, and neither by a curse nor a jest.

He additionally believed we could find strength and courage through religious faith. He wrote in *The Varieties of Religious Experience*, "It makes a tremendous emotional and practical difference to one whether one accepts the universe in the drab discolored way of stoic resignation to necessity, or with the passionate happiness of Christian saints." Faith and hope, therefore, could allow a person to lead a richer, fuller life.

CHAPTER
6

A LASTING LEGACY

I n frail health, William James conducted his last classes at Harvard on January 22, 1907. His students admired James so much that they presented him with a silver loving cup as a sign of their affection. In addition to practicing the values that he suggested in his writings, James took a personal interest in the lives of his family members and students. When one student announced that he was getting married, James invited the young man and his fiancée to his home for dinner and gave them both sound advice about what they could expect.

William James's retirement from teaching at Harvard did not slow down his drive and desire to work. Age and

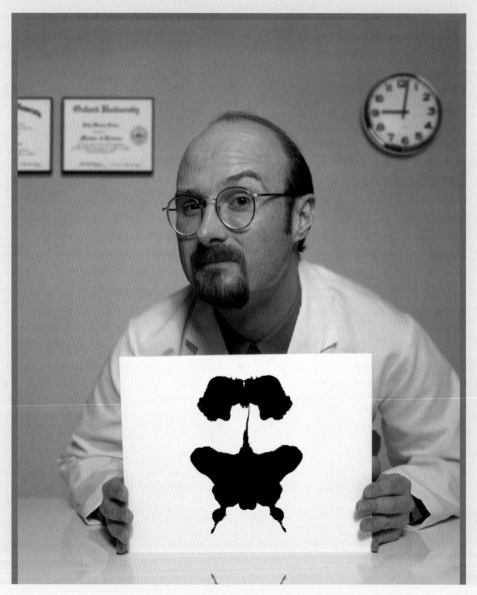

This psychologist is holding up a card from the Rorschach test. During the Rorschach test, a psychiatrist holds up several cards with ink blots on them. A patient tells the psychiatrist what the blots remind him or her of, and the psychiatrist evaluates the answer. Noninvasive psychiatric treatments such as this were rare during James's time, but he helped to develop them.

mounting health problems, especially a failing heart, took their toll on his personal and professional life. Perhaps sensing that the end was near, James seemed to do all that he could to conduct lectures, write, and spread the word about his theories and beliefs.

Just before he retired, James lectured at a number of colleges and universities in the United States, including Wellesley College, the Lowell Institute, and Columbia University. Prior tours of the West Coast, such as stops at the University of California at Berkeley, enabled students to learn of James's work. He compiled the content of these lectures in *Pragmatism*, published the same year as his retirement from Harvard.

In the book, he compares truth to good health. Again, with his own mortality perhaps in mind, he saw the importance of both in life. "Truth" as he saw it could be equated with a person's purpose and will. Just as he believed in the importance of making sound decisions, so too did he believe that once those decisions were made, the individual should pursue the chosen courses with passion and conviction. In *Pragmatism* he wrote that truths "lead us into useful verbal and conceptual quarters as well as directly up to useful sensible termini. They lead to consistency, stability and flowing human intercourse. They lead away from excentricity and isolation, from foiled and barren thinking."

James's view of the truth was, and possibly still is, considered to be radical. He did not think that we are all born with the

John Dewey was a prominent American educator and philosopher whose work revolutionized the way learning takes place in the classroom. Dewey believed students were more likely to learn from participation than memorization. Another pragmatist, Dewey's advances in education are still applied today.

answers to life questions. Instead, he believed that the truth becomes clear to a person only after that individual has gone through life and experienced all that it has to offer—intellectually, to the physical senses, and even through negative experiences. While truths, once found, remained whole, James also felt that such beliefs were like organic, living things that are subject to continual change. For example, he wrote in *Pragmatism* that "beliefs verified concretely by somebody are the posts of the whole superstructure." By superstructure he was referring to that person's belief system.

The publication of *Pragmatism* was followed in 1909 by the release of *A Pluralistic Universe*. This book was based on a series of lectures that he gave at Oxford University. In it, he acknowledged several of his fellow scholars and seemed to want to present his own definition of himself as a philosopher with a "vision." He also suggested that his religious beliefs were strengthening, as he took an even stronger stand on his views of the importance of religious experience in a person's life than he did in his prior book *The Varieties of Religious Experience*. During this later period in his life, he also spoke of his belief in spiritual guidance, mirroring his father's fascination with spirituality.

James had enjoyed a long marriage that produced five children. Despite his own heart troubles, he spent several watchful hours over the sickbed of his novelist brother Henry. Just months later, on August 26, 1910, William James died. His obituary in the *New York Times* began, "Professor William James of Harvard University, America's foremost philosophical writer, virtual founder of the modern school of psychology and exponent of pragmatism, died of heart disease today at his summer home here [New Hampshire]." His legacy, however, continues. His work has had a lasting influence on psychology, science, literature, and American culture.

Thanks to James, America has become one of the world leaders in pioneering treatments for psychological disorders. What began as a struggle with his own tendency toward depression evolved for James into a lifelong study of how the mind works and how its disorders might best be treated. Cures in the nineteenth century, such as removing portions of the brain, electric shock treatments, and administering narcotic drugs, were often horrific and ineffective solutions. James instead offered a gentler approach that later led to psychoanalysis. This method gave health care providers a noninvasive way of studying the thought processes of patients. Psychoanalysis has been used to treat countless patients over the years and continues to be a popular form of treatment.

The work begun by James, Darwin, and other prominent nineteenth-century scientists continues to this day. These men began an investigative line of reasoning that placed emphasis on physical evidence and the fact that organisms are always changing and evolving. Before their views took hold, many people attributed physical or mental illness to demons, bad luck, or other superstitions. James recognized that the brain was an organ not unlike other bodily organs. His work enabled the move of psychology into the medical sciences.

Much of James's work concerned the interrelatedness of all things. Experiences affect other experiences. Thoughts affect other thoughts. People's actions can alter the actions of others. Many scholars believe that James paved the way for

Virginia Woolf was the author of books such as *A Room of One's Own* and *Mrs. Dalloway*. She was a prominent feminist during the late nineteenth and early twentieth centuries. She sometimes used stream of consciousness, which James helped establish, in her fiction. Her books were often experimental and innovative, and would influence many writers that came after her. A page from her notebook *(inset)* shows preliminary notes for her novel *Mrs. Dalloway*.

the discoveries and theories of Albert Einstein (1879–1955), who was the most important physicist of the 1900s and one of the most famous and influential scientists in history. Einstein's work on matter, energy, time, and space followed the general reasoning set forth by James. Einstein's findings have led to current developments concerning the behavior of subatomic particles.

JAMES'S INFLUENCE

American philosopher and educator John Dewey (1859–1952) was greatly influenced by William James and Charles Darwin. Instead of focusing on zoology or religion, Dewey wound up channeling his interests into education. Up until the mid-twentieth century or so, educators believed that memorization was one of the best ways for a student to learn. Dewey, a pragmatist like James, tested out such methods and determined that students learned better when they developed manual skills and when they were allowed to interact with both their teachers and their fellow students. Dewey believed that education should promote a student's mental and physical well-being. This belief was inspired by James's findings that the body and mind operate as one. Many schools implement Dewey's philosophies today.

The term "stream of consciousness," invented by James, is now a standard phrase used by most teachers. It is found in virtually all literature textbooks. The writing technique remains popular to this day for virtually the same reasons that James extolled. It allows readers to hear the thoughts of a character without intrusion from outside events, or input from other characters. Stream-of-consciousness writing can present a pure, unadulterated view of a person's character through his or her thoughts.

William James's focus on the individual and on the terms "me" and "I" in his writings had a profound effect on popular culture. He was one of the first to emphasize self-analysis, introspection, and the importance of each person as a unique entity. This emphasis on the individual would contribute to changes in fashion, clothing, art, music, and other forms of entertainment. Self-expression, then and now, has become a hallmark of American culture.

RELIGION

James saw a difference between organized religion and an individual's personal religious beliefs. The former was linked to culture, tradition, and dogma. The latter was based more on a person's own experiences, be they spiritual or not. Although mysticism and other experimental forms of spirituality existed in the 1800s, the vast majority of people identified with certain organized religions. As the twentieth century went on, that began to change. Now, even if a person belongs to an

James's ideas about American religion were revolutionary in their time, and are still valid today. In this photograph, a family says a prayer before eating dinner together.

established church, that person may have his or her own opinions about church doctrine.

Based on his scientific test subjects and even just conversations with his friends, James observed that people who belonged to an organized religion, or who had some kind of spiritual beliefs that gave them faith and hope, seemed to be happier and more fulfilled. Recent scientific studies have proven these theories to be true. James would never advocate forcing religious views upon anyone, but he did view religion as a possible reliever of stress, depression, and mental anguish.

James also noticed patterns of philosophical and religious thought that occurred during his lifetime. Some periods seemed to be more liberal, while others marked a return to conservatism and to more traditional ways. Those patterns have held out over the past century. Yet again, James was able to theorize on the future by looking at patterns from the past.

POLITICS

The aftermath of the terrorist attacks on September 11, 2001, revealed the tremendous divisions that now exist in the world. The United States has always steadfastly held on to a democratic course, but the nature and application of American democracy have evolved over the years, just as James would have predicted. Conversely, some groups now support extremist religious views and older traditions rooted in their own cultures.

There was controversy during William James's lifetime about America's involvement abroad, particularly in the Philippines. The United States had taken possession of the islands after the Spanish-American War. Filipino guerrilla troops rejected the American presence and declared war against them. As quoted in *Genuine Reality*, James disliked the U.S. government's "abstract war-worship" and feared that the Republican leadership at the time was lapsing into a "deluge of militarism." He told one of his students, "It seems like a regular relapse into savagery."

Instead of war, James preferred to promote discussion and debate. His theories on pragmatism and radical empiricism suggested ways that two very different groups could communicate and come to the best possible solution. Some of these methods were utilized by world leaders when they debated the recent Middle East crisis. James's methods have also been used to resolve academic disputes at universities, and have been applied to the structuring of legal theory for use in criminal courts.

A Return to Jamesian Beliefs?

Few people today could lay claim to the impressive background, education, and achievements of William James. By the age of ten he had traveled to many different countries, read countless books in different languages, and met some of the world's most famous and influential scientists, philosophers, religious leaders, artists, and writers. By the time of his death, he had joined them as someone who had made an impact in the realms of physiology, philosophy, psychology, religion, and science. He was a visionary who not only helped to create advances in these fields, but set the stage for future lines of investigation that are still being pursued today.

William James was a man of his time. During the late 1800s, most well-read people would have been familiar with his name, books, and public lectures. Despite his achievements, he is not as well known today as many of his contemporaries are, possibly because of his gentle approach and the nature of the subjects that he explored. Interest in his work peaked during the late nineteenth and early twentieth centuries, but his global outlook mixed with his sense of independence and individuality still seem very modern and mirror America today.

Currently there is a struggle between globalization and diversity, communalism and the individual. Since James found a balance between all of these perspectives in his life and in his work, perhaps renewed interest in his writings and teachings could provide guidance and healing for the divisions that the United States has experienced in recent years.

TIMELINE

1771 William James Sr., William's grandfather, is born.

1789 William James Sr. emigrates from Ireland to the United States.

1811 Henry James Sr., William's father, is born.

1830s Matthias Schleiden and Theodor Schwann theorize that all living things are made up of individual cells.

1832 William James Sr. dies.

1835 Henry James Sr. enters Princeton Theological Seminary.

1842 William James is born.

1843 William James and his family move to Europe. Henry James Jr. is born.

1848 Alice James is born.

1852 James begins his education in New York.

1855 James begins to receive private tutoring and attends schools in England and France.

1858 James moves back to the United States, and the family settles in Newport, Rhode Island, where James attends school.

1859 James again moves to Europe with his family, where he is schooled and privately tutored in Switzerland and Germany.

1860 James begins to study painting in America.

1861 James enters the Lawrence Scientific School at Harvard University.

1864 James enters Harvard Medical School.

1865 James goes on an expedition to the Amazon in Brazil with scientist Louis Agassiz.

1869 William James receives his medical degree from Harvard Medical School. Dmitri Mendeleyev creates the periodic table of the elements.

1873 James becomes an instructor of anatomy and physiology at Harvard.

1875 James teaches psychology at Harvard and establishes the first ever laboratory of experimental psychology.

1878 James marries Alice Howe Gibbens and begins work on *The Principles of Psychology*.

1879 James begins teaching philosophy at Harvard.

1882 Henry James Sr. dies.

1890 *The Principles of Psychology* is published.

1890–1900 James writes other books and continues to teach, travel, and lecture.

1892 Alice James dies.

1897 James becomes a professor of philosophy at Harvard.

1902 *The Varieties of Religious Experience* is published.

(continued on following page)

(continued from previous page)

1907 *Pragmatism* is published. James teaches his last class at Harvard.

1910 William James dies of heart disease.

1916 Henry James Jr. dies.

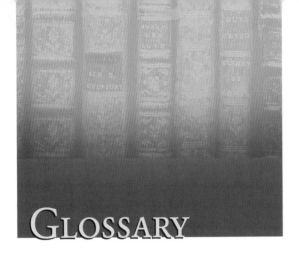

GLOSSARY

aesthetics A branch of philosophy that concerns the nature of beauty, art, and taste.

empiricism The theory that all knowledge comes from experience.

epistemology The study of knowledge and thoughts.

evolution A process described by Charles Darwin in which all living things gradually change over time in response to natural occurrences.

mysticism A movement that believes spiritual truth can be attained through intuitive or paranormal experiences.

natural selection A theory advanced by Charles Darwin, which says that in any given population, those who are the fittest, meaning those who are best suited to their environments, will survive and produce the next generation.

panic attack Feelings of extreme nervousness and unease that strike sufferers often suddenly and without warning. Many members of James's family suffered from such attacks.

philosophy A study of wisdom, values, and reality.

physiology A branch of biology that deals with the study of the physical and chemical processes of the body.

pragmatism A philosophical school that promotes the testing of ideas or opinions based on their utility and consequences.

psychoanalysis A method used in psychology where a patient reveals his or her thoughts in a continuous manner while the health care provider listens to determine patterns and meanings.

psychology The science of mind and behavior.

radical empiricism A school of thought created by William James that holds that knowledge comes from experience, and that experiences can influence both knowledge and other experiences.

Sandemanianism A belief system based on the teachings of Robert Sandeman, who held that all people possessing true faith had an equal chance of being redeemed.

selective consciousness A theory proposed by William James that human consciousness is a force that continuously organizes and controls what it perceives.

stream of consciousness A description created by William James about the way the human mind works; it states that thought consists of disjointed segments strung together in a continuous flow, like a stream.

Swedenborgian theology Beliefs based on the work of Emanuel Swedenborg, who combined mysticism, science, and philosophy.

theology The study of religious faith and experience.

transcendentalism A movement created by thinkers such as Ralph Waldo Emerson; its followers believed spirituality to be more important than the material world.

Victorian Era The term used to describe the sixty-three-year reign of Queen Victoria in England.

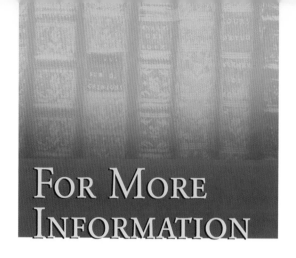

For More Information

The American Philosophical Foundation
31 Amstel Avenue
University of Delaware
Newark, DE 19716-4797
(302) 831-1112
Web site: http://www.apa.udel.edu/apa/index.html

American Philosophical Society
104 South Fifth Street
Philadelphia, PA 19106-3387
(215) 440-3400
Web site: http://www.amphilsoc.org

Cornell University's Making of America
Cornell University
Ithaca, NY 14853
(607) 254-4636
E-mail: info@cornell.edu
Web site: http://www.cornell.edu

Emory University
Division of Educational Studies–William James
1380 Oxford Road
Atlanta, GA 30322
(404) 727-6123
Web site: http://www.des.emory.edu/mfp/james.html

Stanford Encyclopedia of Philosophy
Stanford University
Stanford, CA 94305-2070
(650) 723-2275
Web site: http://plato.stanford.edu/entries/james

Theosophical Society in America
William James, Theosophist
P. O. Box 270
Wheaton, IL 60189-0270
(630) 668-1571
E-mail: olcott@theosmail.net
Web site: http://www.theosophical.org/theosophy/
    questmagazine/novdec2000/lysy

William James Society
University of Arkansas for Medical Sciences
4301 West Markham Street #646
Little Rock, AR 72205

E-mail: jshook@pragmatism.org
Web site: http://www.pragmatism.org/societies/
    william_james.htm

Web Sites

Due to the changing nature of Internet links, the Rosen Publishing Group, Inc., has developed an online list of Web sites related to the subject of this book. This site is updated regularly. Please use this link to access the list:

http://www.rosenlinks.com/lat/wija

FOR FURTHER READING

Feiler, Bruce. *Walking the Bible: An Illustrated Journey for Kids Through the Greatest Stories Ever Told.* New York, NY: Harper Collins Children's Books, 2004.

Fickenscher, Carl. *Faith Alive: The Bible for Lutheran Students.* St. Louis, MO: Concordia Publishing House, 1995.

Goodman, Florence Jeanne. *A Young Person's Philosophical Dictionary: 26 Nouns Which Must Be Known by All Who Would Be Wise and Virtuous.* Los Angeles, CA: Gee Tee Bee, 1978.

Goodtrack, Kim Soo. *ABC's of Our Spiritual Connection.* Penticton, British Columbia: Theytus Books, 1996.

James, William. *Psychology: The Briefer Course.* New York, NY: Dover Publications, 2001.

Kaufman, Gershen, Lev Raphael, and Pamela Espeland. *Stick Up for Yourself: Every Kid's Guide to Personal Power and Positive Self-Esteem.* Minneapolis, MN: Free Spirit Publishing, 1999.

Leone, Bruno. *Creationism Vs. Evolution*. Farmington Hills, MI: Greenhaven, 2001.

Moore Thomas, Shelly. *Somewhere Today: A Book of Peace*. Morton Grove, IL: Albert Whitman, 2002.

Nardo, Don. *Charles Darwin*. Farmington Hills, MI: Thomson Gale, 1999.

Peacock, Judith, and Jackie Casey. *Depression*. Mankato, MN: Capstone Press, 2000.

Sherman, Josepha. *How Do We Know the Nature of the Cell?* New York, NY: Rosen Publishing, 2005.

Singer-Towns, Brian. *The Catholic Youth Bible: New American Bible*. Winona, MN: Saint Mary's Press, 2002.

Ullinskey, Nancy. *Challenges and Choices: Using Creative Stories to Identify and Resolve Middle Grades Issues*. Nashville, TN: Incentive Publications, 1999.

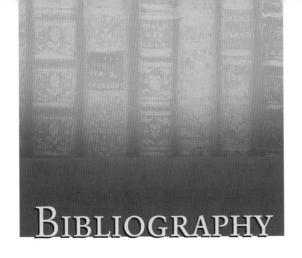

BIBLIOGRAPHY

Aiken, Henry D., and William Barrett. *Philosophy in the Twentieth Century: An Anthology*. Vol. 1. New York, NY: Random House, 1962.

Allen, Gay Wilson. *William James*. New York, NY: The Viking Press, 1967.

Brennan, Bernard P. *William James* (United States Authors). New York, NY: Twayne Publishers, 1968.

Feinstein, Howard M. *Becoming William James*. Ithaca, NY: Cornell University Press, 1984.

Frankel, Charles. *The Golden Age of American Philosophy*. New York, NY: George Braziller, 1960.

James, William. *"The Will to Believe" and Other Essays in Popular Philosophy*. New York, NY: Dover Publications, 1956.

Lewis, R. W. B. *The Jameses: A Family Narrative*. New York, NY: Farrar, Straus and Giroux, 1991.

Menard, Louis. *The Metaphysical Club: A Story of Ideas in America*. New York, NY: Farrar, Straus and Giroux, 2001.

Perry, Ralph Barton. *The Thought and Character of William James.* New York, NY: Harper and Row, 1935.

Ruetenik, Tadd. "Anxiety and Interpretation: Shaping the Experience of William James and Henry James Sr." Retrieved August 9, 2005 (http://www.pragmatism.org/streams/v3n2/anxiety.pdf).

Simon, Linda. *Genuine Reality: A Life of William James.* New York, NY: Harcourt Brace, 1998.

White, Morton. *Science and Sentiment in America.* New York, NY: Oxford University Press, 1972.

INDEX

About the Author

Jennifer Viegas is a news reporter for the Discovery Channel, Animal Planet, TLC: The Learning Channel, and the Australian Broadcasting Corporation. She has written books for the Princeton Review and Random House, and she has also worked as a journalist for ABC News, *New Scientist* magazine, and other publications.

Photo Credits

Cover (portrait), pp. 1, 3, 29, 77 © Getty Images; cover (background), p. 15 © New York Historical Society, New York USA/Bridgeman Art Library; p. 7 Mary Evans Picture Library; pp. 10–11 © James W. Porter/Corbis; pp. 17, 61 © Bettmann/Corbis; p. 19 Princeton Theological Seminary; p. 21 The Art Archive/Gripsholm Castle Sweden/Dagli Orti; p. 23 Book cover reproduced by permission of Oxford University Press, cover painting © Christie's Images, Inc. 1987; pp. 25, 37, 39 © North Wind Picture Archives; p. 31 © Time-Life Pictures/Getty Images; p. 34 National Portrait Gallery, Smithsonian Institution/Art Resource, N.Y.; pp. 41, 86 The New York Public Library/Art Resource, N.Y.; pp. 46, 54, 75, 89 (left) Library of Congress Prints and Photographs Division; p. 48 © Allen Ginsberg/Corbis; p. 51 © Tom Boyle/ Getty Images; p. 64 NARA; p. 68 Gogh, Vincent van (1853–1890), *The Starry Night.* 1889. Oil on canvas, 29 x 36¼". Acquired through the Lillie P. Bliss Bequest. (472.1941) Location: The Museum of Modern Art, New York, NY, U.S.A. Photo Credit: Digital Image © The Museum of Modern Art/Licensed by SCALA/Art Resource, NY; p. 71 General Research Division, The New York Public Library, Astor, Lenox and Tilden Foundations; pp. 79, 81 © AFP/ Getty Images; p. 84 ©Phil Bunko/Getty Images; p. 89 (right) British Library/ HIP/Art Resource; p. 92 Tom Stewart/Corbis.

Designer: Gene Mollica; **Editor:** Nicholas Croce
Photo Researcher: Marty Levick